Through Her Voice

DEDICATION

This one is for Mama Scratch. Meow.

ACKNOWLEDGMENTS

I would like to thank my family, Ben, Lori, all of my amazing friends from writers' group, Pumpkin, all of the "nice" people I was friends with in high school including the ones who metaphorically stabbed me in the back, (thanks for the inspiration), and the Fates.

PHOTO CREDITS
Cover and About the Author photos by
Ben Eisenkraft

Through Her Voice

By Samantha Apicella

Friday, September 3rd

Nothing is sacred.

Rusty is fingering a bag of weed in his jeans pocket as elderly Mr. Rodman attempts to teach us about old western outlaws.

Mr. Rodman is an interesting dude though.

As I write in this journal as I do almost every class, I seem to be the only one paying attention.

A shame isn't it?

Rusty can care less. His bloodshot eyes, deteriorating band t-shirt, and deep chocolate pupils say it all.

Ha, ha what a stoner...

My upright posture, perfectly lined cat eyes, and my vigorous "notes" of Mr. Rodman's lecture tell a story of their own.

Nothing is as it seems.

It never is.

The bell rings.

Mr. Rodman scratches his head and is probably wondering where all the time has gone; or maybe his head was just itchy.

Rusty storms out of last period and into the hallways with his crew of lost boys. They make suggestive gestures to Rusty, all giggling in unison.

As Rusty and the other lost boys exit to get their "escape on" he turns around and stares directly into my eyes.

An uncontrollable grin is planted on my lips for a millisecond.

An unwanted grin.

Rusty's eyes are pleading for salvation. His actions say otherwise.

I quickly look away in remembrance of the past.

Let that smoke swallow that waste alive.

I pull my notebooks closer to my chest and tell Mr. Rodman to have a good weekend like the nerdy, innocent girl I am. He nods, says "thanks", and wishes me the same. Then, he weakly strolls away putting on a fedora. He holds open the main exit door for about ten students.

None say "thank you."

I stop writing and walk away.

Homework awaits.

Rusty's Personal Journal - Sunday, September 5th

Dude I don't even know how or why I am writing in this thing right now... but I am. This weekend was fucking insane. Like you would think it's the beginning of the new school year, let's get to work.

But nah, I had one hell of a weekend. It started after school Friday.

Oh man let me tell you.

There were five minutes left in Rodman's class. My boys kept texting me to meet them out back behind the dumpsters. They kept saying they got this new shit that I had to try. I was just thinking I wanna smoke some bud! Get me outta this class!

So anyway, I get out there to not only find a nice, fat one waiting for me but that blonde bitch that used to be friends with my ex was standing there with her fat ass friend.

So then I said to my boys right in front of her 'cuz I don't care, I was like, "Dude what the hell is she doing here?"

Then she was like, "What's the problem, Rusty? I'm the one who brought this shit. I should be allowed to partake."

Then I replied with, "Well what's so special about it anyway?"

Then she said, "Smoke up and you'll find out."

This was when things got weird.

I got so high from whatever kind of weed that was. But it wasn't a good high. Dude, I wouldn't be surprised if she had roofied me. The next thing I knew I was in this chick's house in her room and we were hooking up, no sex, just hardcore making out. And before I can tell her to get her grimy body off of me, she starts pulling down my jeans, yanking off my boxers, and whipping my junk out.

"Uh where did my boys go?" I asked with intoxicated confusion.

"Who cares?" She giggled while taking off her bra. "Let's have fun."

And being me, I was too high to object to this not so fun but fun activity. She's one of those girls that you use and throw away. Don't get me wrong. I am not a misogynist. I just took advantage of the opportunity that presented itself to me.

Then there was Saturday night. The Spoiled Tulips were playing a show at the beach. The only good thing about living here is our local rock scene. And you can get hella high without anyone bothering you about it.

So there I was at the beach with my boys starting a nice mosh pit on the sand while Spoiled Tulips played. I had heard Kiedis, their lead singer, was throwing a basement party after. My boys and I were so there after the show. We were getting pumped in the pit as practice for later.

But anyway, in the midst of this utter chaos, something brought my focus away from the pit. My ex was staring at me outside of the crowd and near the brush. The moment I stared back she looked away and was writing something down in this notebook I always see her carrying around. It's kind of weird. Ever since we broke up she's been a loner with her notebook by her side, like that thing is her new best friend.

Monday, September 6th

As they say, "to each their own".

This weekend was like most others I've experienced; except this time, I found myself on a higher path to realization, knowledge.

The Spoiled Tulips were playing at the beach on Saturday.

Naturally, I attended this pathetic excuse for an alternative rock show.

Alone.

Not lonely; rather, alone.

The sun had just begun to set towards the lake's shallow horizon.

The sky had morphed into a psychedelic blend of fuchsia and creamy orange. A hot sky meant a scorching tomorrow...

The sky looked so untouched, so natural, so stunning.

I closed my eyes imagining the taste of the sky.

Soft.

Fluffy.

Untouched.

The familiar smell of marijuana made me come down from the sky, back to reality.

Rusty was offering me a drag.

"You know I don't smoke."

"Whatever."

The waste walked into the thorny brush away from the lake. The other lost boys followed.

Zombies, all of them.

But I was here for the music.

The Spoiled Tulips are a very generic-sounding indie band; but their repetitive bass lines sucked me in at that moment. The music surrounded my being.

I didn't need weed.

I didn't need piercings.

I didn't need tattoos.

I didn't need pills.

I didn't need a boyfriend.

And I certainly didn't need "friends".

I had my music.

It spoke to me.

We laughed, rejoiced, felt.

We didn't abandon.

Trust, the music and I.

Nothing else mattered.

But he kept catching my gaze. He was singing the songs, effortlessly strumming the chords to my heart.

He was Kiedis.

I was there for the music, not him. He was just another boy.

What had mattered at that moment was the music; but what matters now, as I'm writing this, is the quick eating of my lunch so I can get a head start on my homework for tonight and ignore Ugly Girl kissing Rusty a table over.

Ugly Girl died a long time ago. She used to be my best friend.

Later

Homework and music, homework and music,
homework and music, dinner, homework and
music, Father Monster yelling at Mother,
Sister's rap music, social media, coffee
with Mom, television, sleep.

Wednesday, September 8th

Wednesdays are stupid.

You're halfway through your weekdays and closer to the weekend, middle ground.

I eat lunch in my choral teacher's room in solitude.

I can't stand that cafeteria lately.

So noisy.

So untamed.

So juvenile.

Here, I could think without distractions.

No lost boys.

No Ugly Girl.

No Rusty.

Negativity is unseen.

I can write in silence.

Ignorance is bliss.

But when I really think about it, I think, what is so great about the weekend?

I'm not gaining anything by it really.

In school, I'm furthering myself both mentally and physically.

At home, all I hear is Monster roaring.

I don't really have a father. I have a monster.

But then there's Mom.

So beautiful.

So comforting.

So understanding.

So rad.

My mom is a strong lady. After all, she deals with a grotesque monster every day. And she gave birth to the monster's two intelligent daughters.

The weekdays suck for most teenagers.

But for me, the weekdays are my weekends.

Solution, appreciation, vacation, I rejoice.

Rusty's Personal Journal - Thursday, September 9th

So I guess the blonde chick is my girlfriend now. I was probably stoned when she asked for approval of our new label.

Whatever.

Everyone knows high school couples never last.

But I do recall one thing that happened yesterday. We were eating lunch in the café, (my boys made weed brownies), and my girlfriend was being mad clingy. She kept trying that PDA shit on me.

How would you feel if someone unappealing kept sticking their tongue down your throat?

My boys think she's so hot. I feel like telling them that they can have her. I mean she's pretty much a skank.

But then I see my ex by herself again with that fucking journal like two tables over. And I am kind of intrigued. I mean I think it's weird that she is always alone; but what I really want to know is what is so special about that damn journal?!

Then my skanky girlfriend was like, "What are you looking at, babe?"

Then I was like, "Nothing."

And then she realized. "Oh, you mean her." She gestured to my ex. I didn't reply.

Then she was like, "I know. She's fun to

laugh at. Let's go back to your house."

And then we did.

Oh crap, I had thought. This is the first time she's meeting my parents. She was wearing a crop top, belly ring out (which is hot but skanky), and jeans with probably the biggest rips I have ever seen.

When my mom got first glance, she went pale. My dad was still at work.

My mom was like, "Rusty, who's she?"

I almost pissed my pants trying to contain my laughter.

Then I proclaimed, "Hey mom, this is my girlfriend."

I love pissing my parents off.

My girl had to run to the bathroom. That was when mom had it with me.

She angrily whispered, "Rusty, I don't know what you're thinking. It looks like she's been around the block ten times!"

Then I said, "Mom, it's all good. We aren't having sex."

Then I walked away and got the bong ready in my room.

Friday, September 10th

We're all weirdos.

It's true.

We all have flaws no matter how perfect someone seems.

Don't ever be fooled.

It's yet another Friday evening, almost the dreaded weekend.

And I have nothing to do but write in this journal and drink tea down at the coffeehouse.

There are other young people at the coffeehouse...

With friends.

Laughing.

Blocks of light shining in each of their bronzed faces.

Electronic light.

Guidos, guidettes.

Smiling like madmen.

Happy as a drunk.

Think about that.

Then there's the porch. I see the usual clouds of smoke rising under the fluorescent coffeehouse lights. They're doing just the same minus a few electronic lights and bronzed skin.

The regulars.

The coffeehouse people are rad to talk to. Some are even my friends.

It's my home away from home. We're like family. We're so comfortable with each other that we don't need any formal greetings or conversations, just freedom.

And we're all individuals, each and every one of us.

And in comes Ugly Girl with her gruesome best friend, Miss Oink.

They freeze like the Antarctic when they see me. Ugly Girl and Miss Oink are truly ignorant creatures. How did they not expect to see me here?

This is my turf, not theirs.

Whatever, I don't care.

Everyone here knows they're disgusting creatures. Just looking at them gives indication as harsh as it may sound.

I speak the truth no matter how harsh it is.

Ugly Girl and Miss Oink are only immature and were in the way of my path to enlightenment.

Woo-hoo.

My hippy friend, Jive, just came in from the porch.

"The Spoiled Tulips are having a last minute show tonight at the beach. You in?

We're leaving now."

"Sure," I say with a smile.

This is perfect.

I can talk to Kiedis this time.

He's an individual.

He's different.

Adios, creature girls!

As I depart my home away from home, the sun begins to set.

But this time, the sky doesn't look yummy.

The sky is turning into a static picture on a television set: dark, pixelated, and showing no illustration.

Sunday, September 12th

The Spoiled Tulips show was a good time... except I never got to talk to Kiedis.

Maybe it was because of me spending time watching my coffeehouse friends smoke cigarettes; maybe because of all the girls and groupies talking to Kiedis; maybe because of all the hits he took from his bong before the band performed; or maybe because under those long, chestnut locks and pouty lips there lays a stoner, a criminal, a loser.

But who knows?

Do I really have the ability to sense these things without even knowing someone?

Maybe I was scared or maybe just wise.

Time will tell.

In other news, Father Monster has been spitting lava out of his rancid mouth all weekend. The splatters of lava burned Mom, me, and even Sister, though she appears happy.

Repression is aggression which leads to depression.

I am a prisoner in my own home.

Father Monster may incinerate us if we leave.

Music is my escape.

The art.

The sounds.

The literature.

It's my euphoric haze.

Set me free, escape, amaze me.

Rusty's Personal Journal - Monday, September 13th

So this weekend my parents took me and my little bro, Frankie, up to the lake house. I hate going there. It's in the middle of nowhere and I'm stuck with my parents and perfect 10 year old, Frankie.

The first thing that happens when we get there is Frankie wants to go swimming. That lake is so grimy. There's this dock out in the middle that all the kids love to swim to and jump off of.

This dock is littered with dead fish guts among other unmentionables such as used condoms and sometimes even dead birds.

But for some odd fucking reason, it doesn't bother Frankie in the least.

So I was like, "Mom, I'm not taking him to that dock. It's disgusting."

Then of course she was like, "Rusty, do this for your brother. You have nothing better to do anyway."

Then my father has to add on the usual, "It'll distract you from those unhealthy habits of yours."

I just shook my head and took perfect Frankie down to the dock.

And that's the problem I have with my parents. They assume I have nothing better to do than smoke weed and hang out with so-called "degenerates." What they don't understand is that those "degenerates" are

my friends. And I have plenty more to do
than smoke.

After all, they don't know about this
journal or the fact that I came to school
high today.

Right now, I'm in the library listening
to some music.

My ex is looking at me with doe eyes.

Thursday, September 16th

Zombie morning.

Zombie school.

Mr.Rodman's lecture.

Homework and music.

Homework and music.

Dinner with the family and Father Monster.

Coffeehouse (I saw Rusty there with his lost boys.)

Social media.

Sleep.

Redundancy.

Living it up zombie style.

Rusty's Personal Journal - Thursday, September 16th

It's almost midnight and I can't sleep. I wake up at 6 AM tomorrow for a place I find to be useless. It's been a long day.

I come home to find my mom and dad sitting at the kitchen table with these creepy grins on their faces. They were waiting for me. Dad's never home early from work. I was beginning to wonder again if my girl had drugged me.

So I was like, "Why's he home early?"

Then my dad answered with, "We have some exciting news for you, Rusty."

I rolled my eyes. I knew this was yet another attempt to get me off the herb as my parents like to call it. But before I could object, my over-eager mother said it.

"Dad talked to a few coaches at your school and convinced them to let you back onto the varsity baseball team. Isn't that great?!"

No, I thought. That is not fucking great. I won't have time for anything, no friends, no girls, no music, no weed, no pills, no chill time. I was pissed. I had to say something.

"Why would I want to go back on that damn team?" I asked them both trying not to yell. "Why would you do this behind my back?!"

Then my dad responded with the usual, "Rusty, you were one of the best on that team. It's a shame you got kicked off to begin with."

Then my mom was all like, "It's for your own good, honey. It's a healthy activity."

She emphasized the word healthy. I just shook my head and told them I was going out for the night. When they asked where, I slammed the front door and began to text my boys for plans.

And then we went to the coffeehouse in town. We smoked a little on the way. I took some heavy hits off the joint we were passing.

I was good for the rest of the night. Fuck my parents.

But then my anger subsided for a minute. I saw my ex sitting at the corner table as we walked in. She was reading a book of poems. And of course that journal was on the table too. She was sipping some tea from a porcelain cup… porcelain like her skin, so soft.

My girl's skin isn't very soft.

She was wearing a black, lacy dress with pink Doc Martens. There's always something mysterious about her, something undefinable.

But then she noticed I was looking and took her books and tea to a table outside. I looked back at the menu and wondered why she was running away.

My anger towards my parents suddenly vanished. I was distracted.

Friday, September 17th

Fate is my guide.

And here we are again. It's Friday.

There's no Spoiled Tulips show tonight, which means no talking to Kiedis.

I added him on Facebook yesterday.

He automatically accepted my friend request, which is rad I guess... Though he may just accept everyone.

The coffeehouse cow clock reads 7:31 PM. And the regulars are here along with the guidos and guidettes. My sister's also working her shift.

I'm drinking my tea.

Writing.

Venting.

Creating.

Thinking.

My birthday is in a few weeks or so. I want to go to a real, antique haunted house this year, a real one. I want all of the regulars to be there too. I want there to be candlelight and warmth emanating from the presence of my lost friends around me.

And as for gifts, I have only one request:

him.

Does he really exist?

Am I always going to be alone?

He's a real man with substance, form, smooth texture, beauty, intelligence, and goals.

Rusty, for example, is the one type of individual that I do not want. Rusty is a stoner who does nothing to put his aspirations into effect. He simply doesn't care. His mind is on the herb aka his love aka his drugs.

Ugly Girl is failing at trying to make me jealous. Ugly Girl is a sad fool who doesn't know what she wants herself.

Maybe we're all fools, sad or not.

Bing!

Long, chestnut hair, unique aqua eyes, and a tall, lanky figure walks into the coffeehouse.

Alone.

Fate walks in.

And I greet Fate with a smile.

My curiosity awaits Fate.

Later...Midnight

Kiedis and I spoke.

"Are you two twins?" he asked pointing at my sister and me.

"No," I replied getting up from my chair. "But everyone says that. I'm the older one actually."

And we introduced ourselves.

"Yeah, I was at a few of your shows already. The last one I was hanging out with Jive."

"Mhm," he answered.

That's all he said. Oh, and this:

"Well, I'm gonna head outside to have some cigs. See you around."

That was the conversation between Kiedis and me.

Beauty isn't everything.

As a Libra, I strive to achieve balance, which does not include hitting bongs and smoking cigs with groupies.

Rusty's Personal Journal - Saturday, September 18th

So my family took me apple picking today. I hate this time of the year. And I don't understand why my parents keep making me do shit with them. I love my little bro and all, but every time I'm with him I notice how much my parents seem to cherish him.

How come they never do that with me? I guess because I'm not fucking perfect like cute, little Frankie. It just makes me feel like crap about myself.

At least it gets me away from my skanky girlfriend. She keeps telling me she wants to have sex. There's no way that's gonna happen. I'd rather have sex with a dog than even think of doing that with her.

I mean like I'm not a virgin anymore. I haven't been since my ex and I broke up. And I'm not proud of how I lost it either.

But I'll save that story for another time. I'm gonna go smoke a bowl.

Rusty's Personal Journal - Sunday, September 19th

Even though baseball season is almost over, I had to go to the school gym today at five in the fucking morning for a two hour workout.

Why are my parents making me do this? Even if I'm good at it, that doesn't mean I like it. Oh yeah, and there are monthly drug tests.

Lucky for me there are only gonna be two since the season, like I said, is close to being over.

So basically all morning, I've been asking people who don't smoke to give me their pee in a bottle. This is mad hard. Basically everyone I chill with smokes. I have until tomorrow after school.

Dude this sucks.

Monday, September 20th

This has been a weird day so far.

A surprise greeted me on the way to class. I'm just minding my business, putting my jacket and backpack into my locker and as I shut my locker door, he scares the crap out of me.

"Oh my god," I said taken aback, nearly dropping all of my books. "Rusty, where did you come from?"

"Not important," he said quickly while looking back and forth. "Can I have your pee in this bottle? I'll pay you."

"What?" I answer in utter disgust. "Why? That's just weird. I'm not doing that."

"20 bucks," Rusty pleaded with me as I turned to walk away.

"No," I said shaking my head.

I don't even know why I dated him.

Rusty's Personal Journal - Monday, September 20th

I'm so lucky. Some nerd in my history class took my money and gave it to me. Success. I am seriously pissed at my parents for making me have to go through this shit. That was seriously intense man.

Now it's 6 PM and I'm sitting in my room. My girlfriend just called and wanted to know if I can come over. I said okay. But I think tonight I need to tell her we're done. I'm not gonna be some dick who breaks up with a girl over the phone. I'm gonna tell it to her face and be like, "Listen, this isn't working."

I can't wait for this day to be over.

Monday, September 20th (later)

It's 9 PM. The night tends to bring on deep thoughts for me. I am listening to this band that broke up a few years ago. I wish they never did. Their music makes me think.

It also blocks out the sound of Father Monster screaming at my mother for lying about her personal email password. He demands and demands and demands to see it. He wants to see her personal email, read every message, every word.

Here are Father Monster's thoughts: *That cunt is cheating on me. She's fucking that old high school buddy of hers. That's why she has this email. That's why she hid the password from me, that lying whore.*

This is real life people. And guess what? Father Monster speaks those thoughts, those vile, psychotic, irrational thoughts. He broadcasts them for the entire block to hear. People tend to turn the other cheek. They are all self-righteous sheep.

And through the music I just heard him smash her laptop. What else is new? But it still hurts. It's like why do those who you think are there for you or are supposed to be never are?

Ugly Girl and Miss Oink betrayed me. Rusty broke my heart. And what's worse is I don't have a father.

Life is ironic indeed.

Rusty's Personal Journal - Tuesday, September 21st

I did it. It was a mess. If our break-up was a fight scene from an action film, blood would be splattered all over the walls. That's how much of a mess it was.

So I'm at her house. Her mom answers the door and directs me to her bedroom. I walk in to find my girl posed on her twin size mattress in a corset and thong. The worst part of her ensemble was the heart-shaped whip she was clasping in her right hand.

"Rusty," she sang staying in her seductive, yet totally hilarious pose. "Tonight is the night I conquer you."

Dude, I thought. *You cannot go through with this. Your first time was shitty enough. Don't let your second time be another regret.*

"Listen," I said looking directly into her horny eyes. "We need to talk."

"Come sit down," she said patting her mattress. "Tell me all about your problems. I can fix them." She winked.

I had to just say it. So I did.

"This isn't working," I said nervously running my fingers through my mess of hair.

"No worries," she giggled. "I'll ditch the whip."

Shit, this isn't going to be easy, I thought.

"No, I mean we aren't working. I think it's time for us to see other people."

There was a brief silence. Then she sat up. The storm was brewing. I felt it.

"So are you actually breaking up with me right now?" She asked incredulously with her hands on her hips.

"Um… yeah I am. I'm sorry. I just feel like we want different things right now."

Oh no, the storm arrived. She started bawling.

"So I'm not good enough for you?! Is that what you're saying?!"

"No, no, it's not that. It's…"

"Get out!" She yelled through tears. "After all of the weed I gave you, you stab me in the back. You used me. You're disgusting, you fucking trashy stoner. Get out now!"

And so I left. I feel relieved. And now it's time to actually do some of Rodman's homework. He's been loading on a lot lately.

Dude, I can't have my parents on my back anymore. I have to do this shit. Write you in a bit. Peace.

Monday, October 4th

"I don't think they were really evil," I stated to Mr. Rodman and the rest of the unaroused class.

"Yes, they committed crimes; but maybe the outlaws were just misunderstood by society and judged because of the propaganda surrounding them. Signs all over the country that read "Wanted Dead Or Alive" might have aided in this judgment people had placed on them. Who actually knew Billy the Kid as a real person anyway?"

Mr. Rodman was speechless along with the rest of the class.

I thought I had actually stumped everyone. That was until a hand was raised from the back of the room near the door.

"Yes, Rusty?" Mr. Rodman nodded to the stoner.

Rusty never participated in class. Where had this come from?

"I second that," Rusty said with conviction. "Except those dudes were only trying to make a statement to the country. What is considered to be the "norm" sucks and always will. There's nothing wrong with shaking up the system."

I turned around to face the now grinning stoner ready for rebuttal. That grin brought up too many memories in my mind.

"But Rusty, there's definitely something wrong with killing innocent others. That makes them criminals, not system shakers."

"Okay," he replied rolling his sparkling brown eyes. "But I thought you just said not to judge others. How do you know these innocents were really innocent?"

I felt my cheeks getting red partially from annoyance; and the other part from... I didn't even want to admit.

"Well, did you know Billy the Kid? Maybe he's your long lost relative. I mean, you act a lot like him, doing drugs, screwing girl after girl, and vandalizing any chance you can get."

"Maybe, I'll be famous one day then," said Rusty crossing his arms. "While you're a sad, old cat lady with nothing to live for except the ghost of your dead husband."

"That's enough!" Mr. Rodman exclaimed.

I never heard Mr. Rodman yell like that before. I was now speechless.

"You and Rusty better see me after class."

Later

And that brings me to now.

3 PM after school outside in the pouring rain picking up litter from the faculty parking lot wearing disgusting neon orange ponchos... with Rusty.

This is just wonderful.

Empty gum pack.

Water bottle.

A winter glove.

A pencil.

A paper bag.

Disregarded.

Who knows where these things came from?

What have they been through to get to this spot, in the pouring rain on the hard ground?

Alone.

"Cover for me," said Rusty walking towards the back entrance of the school. "I'm going to smoke a j. Tell Rodman I had the craps."

Are. You. Serious?!

"No, no, no," I replied running after Rusty, grabbing his soft hand. "I'm not covering for you or doing the rest of this on my own. You're the one who got me into this mess, so you're staying."

"Whatever," he mumbled breaking away from my hand and continuing for the door.

"No," I said as I jumped in front of it. "You're staying. Smoke your j later."

He looked straight into my cat eyes at that moment. My cheeks were turning red again, but not from anger.

This is exactly how he used to look at me when we were swimming in love, in sweetness, in passion... together.

Rusty hasn't looked at me since then, eight months ago, until now.

"Okay," Rusty said as he went back to work.

He stabbed the empty water bottle as he continued to stare into my soul.

Rusty's Personal Journal - Monday, October 4th

Dude, I don't know what it is; but it's like my ex has this power over me. I wanted to smoke so badly. I mean I am now, but that's because I'm home. Detention sucked. We picked up some trash in the faculty parking lot.

What does that teach anyone? Clean up other people's messes while wearing some ridiculous poncho thing?

Whoa, this weed is really making me think today. My dealer must be getting better shit.

Or maybe I am.

Wednesday, October 6th

There's no such thing as normal.

But it was a pretty usual day for me.

School was the same as always. Rusty doesn't acknowledge me; Ugly Girl and Miss Oink snicker every time I walk past them; and Mr. Rodman gives a bad ass lecture as always.

At home, Father Monster continues to spread his rage and psychosis.

"Why did you go to the mall today you lazy, fat whore?! DID YOU GO TO FUCK YOUR BOYFRIEND???" He slams the door to his monster cave.

Mom goes back upstairs appearing numb to the abuse even though I know she isn't.

Sister continues to blast her head-pounding music.

Mom and I talk about how much we wish we could get rich and take a road trip to California.

As the crescent moon above begins to get clearer as the sky turns to onyx nightfall, my family falls into slumber.

I'm sleepy myself; but I decide to log onto Facebook. I get a message from Kiedis. He wants to see a movie with me Friday night. I say, "I'd love to."

Game on.

Rusty's Personal Journal - Friday, October 8th

This is gonna be my chill night. The boys asked me to hang out but I told them nah. Baseball practices have been knocking me out.

I'm sore like all over. The weed helps with the pain a bit. But it's not all the hype all those pro-marijuana people speak of. It's still fun though.

I figured that now is the moment I will tell you about my first time. I'm bored and why the hell not?

This is how it happened.

It was like eight months ago right after I broke up with my then girlfriend. I'm a teenage male... you know, I get urges. My mind was all fucked up from the break-up. So I go to some random party happening at my boy Steve's house that night.

I get there all depressed and Steve was like, "Yo man, I got some dank shit to cheer you up."

He has this massive bong set up on his living room table. The place was packed. A lot of people looked older. I didn't give a shit. I didn't question the bong. I just did what I was told. I smoked a lot of weed.

And just when I was starting to come down from the high like an hour or two later Steve comes up with some tall blonde chick with breast implants, dread locks, and tattoos covering her arms. Her lips looked implanted too. She was like a stoner's dream, really sexy.

"Rusty, this is my cousin Daisy," Steve said with a big grin.

"Enchanted," Daisy said batting her eyelashes. She took my hand and kissed it leaving a red lipstick stain behind. She smelt like cherry chap stick and looked like a stripper for sure.

That was when Steve pulled me aside. And whispered the following in my ear: "Wanna get laid? She's your girl."

Then he slipped me a tiny, unknown pill.

"Take this and thank me later." Then he walked away.

Once again, I didn't think and did what I was told.

The next thing I knew I was in Steve's bedroom and Daisy was straddling me, taking her top off, then mine. Her tits were very big, very sexy, and very fake.

So in a daze I asked her, "How old are you anyway?"

And then she giggled and was like, "21."

I started laughing like a drugged idiot, which I totally was. And then without realizing it I felt her putting the condom on. And like two minutes later it was done. And she was gone. Then I passed out on Steve's bed.

When I woke up, it was 3 AM. I was so

fucked. Literally.

I ran home to find my furious and worried parents who wouldn't let me out of the house again for a few months.

But that didn't stop me. I kept buying weed from Steve, who I still buy from to this day. And I still hung out with stoners. And I still can't fully remember my first time.

That's the worst part.

Friday, October 8th

As I've said, nothing is as it seems.

Ironically, it never struck me as odd that Kiedis asked me to the movies out of the blue...

until now.

I'm a paranoid person.

I always question everything, good or bad.

But I really didn't want to question Kiedis' intentions.

Maybe I'm overthinking things like I usually do...

maybe.

Kiedis is my song; and I want his song to make me smile.

Wish me luck.

Saturday, October 9th

I honestly don't know what to think about last night.

The date definitely wasn't one I've dreamt of; but it wasn't a total shipwreck either.

I met Kiedis at the movie theater.

Though, we didn't have very much time for talking. This was due to the fact that Kiedis arrived to the theater late and stoned.

The movie was nothing special, just a typical action adventure flick that involved a bomb, a helpless female hostage, and a drug trade of sorts.

Kiedis loved it, maybe because he was stoned.

Those types of movies are targeted towards all of the Kiedises out there.

Anyway, after the typical movie, Kiedis wanted to do something not so typical for a first date: hang out in his car.

I was tempted to say no.

I wanted to say no.

But when I turned to face him, something made my insides flutter.

His eyes were a glassy, hypnotic shade of blue.

His pouty lips seemed sexier.

"Sure," I answered in a dream-like haze.

He smiled back at me and grabbed my hand in response.

When we got to his beat-up burgundy SUV, I floated inside to the cold leather of the passenger's seat that awaited my little booty.

A smell of weed, cigarettes, and vomit automatically entered my nostrils. A normally gross combination of scents became non-existent to me.

I suddenly felt tingly all over. I was in a drunken state of mind; yet I hadn't had anything to drink. I don't know what had come over me; but I didn't care.

I was hand in hand with Kiedis, the guy who sang the songs to my heart.

Fingers continuously intertwined, we spoke about our lives, our favorite bands, our friends, our interests.

His favorite color is tie-dye.

He loves his dog, Bella, and his weed of course.

Conversation was flowing.

Then there was silence.

Yes, the actual sound of silence.

It exists.

His hand broke away from mine. His fingers began to trail down my waist and tickled my thigh. I looked up at him. He stared back at me. And with his other hand, he lightly held my chin up. I shifted closer to him until our lips made contact and had a conversation of their own. His tongue looped around mine like a rollercoaster, fast and so totally reckless. The hand that held my thigh soon made its way to my back and began to explore under my shirt.

I shivered.

This. Felt. Too. Reckless.

"Kiedis," I broke away from his grip. "This is our first date. We barely know each other."

"Okay, I actually respect that," he replied in a surprisingly understanding tone. "Want me to walk you back to your car?"

I nodded yes.

He walked me back under the parking lot spotlights.

"Thanks," I said once we stopped a few feet from my car.

He grabbed me by the waist and drew me close to his skinny but warm body and gave me a delicate yet euphoric kiss goodnight.

I felt like flying to my car. Kiedis' kiss made me feel so light, so free.

But all of a sudden, I was grounded back. The sight of Ugly Girl and Miss Oink sitting on the sidewalk across from my car returned me to reality.

Haters.

They were having their own conversation and didn't seem to notice my presence.

But they had.

As I approached the driver's door, a sticky note that read, "slut", was stuck onto the window.

I apathetically peeled it up, threw it to the cement, and drove away.

Rusty's Personal Journal- Sunday, October 10th

Life is funny shit, man. And oh yeah Sundays suck. I just went on Facebook and found something weird. My ex went on a date with that moron Kiedis from the Spoiled Tulips, LOL. Oh man.

I guess that's chill for her and all, but Kiedis is a pure-bred stoner. I thought she was against all of that. I mean for real, I've seen that dude in action at parties and let me tell you, he's always high on acid.

My boys think I'm jealous.

Funny shit, man.

Monday, October 11th

Girls are like mosquitoes. They swarm around your body, nipping at your delicate skin attempting to suck the sweet, red liquid out of it. They always sniff out the sweetest blood;

their sustenance;

their nectar;

their target.

But what mosquitoes don't seem to understand is that they can easily be squashed.

Mosquitoes are simply miniscule, thirsty insects in this crazy world.

As I approach my locker this morning, I find yet another sticky note. This one reads: "He's not into you… slut." There is also a crusty lip gloss stain on the note… ew.

The note itself doesn't even bother me. It's just the fact that I touched Ugly Girl's lip stains.

I crumple up the nonsense and throw it in the nearest trash can.

Ugly Girl is one jealous, insecure creature. She's just thirsty for a fight to replace her lack of love from anyone of the opposite sex. She's always been a jealous creature.

English class awaits.

Life goes on.

Later

It's now lunch.

I'm eating in my choral teacher's room as always.

And I've remembered something.

My birthday is in three days.

What am I going to do on such an occasion? I still want to go to a haunted house. Maybe I'll just play it safe and go to the one at the amusement park that I love... Or maybe, I'll shake up the system this year.

Time will tell.

Rusty's Personal Journal - Tuesday, October 12th

Steve picked me up this morning and I got what I needed for today:

my little yellow pill.

Everything has been stupid lately. Frankie got an award from his teacher for having the best spelling test grades in the class.

Then I have baseball practice practically every morning. And my parents still give me no recognition.

And let's not forget Her.

My ex is driving me crazy and I have no fucking clue why. It's not like we talk besides detention recently picking up garbage. Maybe it's Kiedis. That dude pisses me off.

I think it's the fact that she left me for him.

No wait… I broke up with her. Dude, I'm way too tired.

Thank God for my little yellow pill.

Thursday, October 14th (My Birthday)

In a way, birthdays are pretty depressing. You're another year closer to death.

But gifts are fun. Being with your family is supposed to be fun.

My relatives are coming over tonight for my birthday cake. I am utterly cringing at this very thought.

I wonder if Father Monster will be on his best behavior tonight for the festivities... Let's hope he puts on a good show. Or maybe it's better if everyone sees his true colors.

On Facebook I received 38 birthday wishes. 38 is my lucky number. It's always appearing in my life. 38 seems like an excessive number of birthday wishes for someone like me though. I only have a small group of friends.

Why do people insist on being so fake?

They don't really care.

No one cares about anyone in this world, besides Mom of course, and myself.

Rodman's class is chill today. He put on a gangster movie for us to watch. Rusty left for the bathroom before and has not come back. Rodman looks like he's about to fall asleep. His white beard has pieces of bread crumbs in it, probably from a sandwich.

I have seen this movie way too many times to actually pay any attention to it anymore.

Dream-like thoughts are flying through my mind about tomorrow night. I'm going to the haunted house down in the city by the waterfront. Jive had suggested it. I have never been to this one; so I'm excited. I love the gory theatrics.

When I was little, those theatrics scared me. Now, they are a means of escape and fun...

Oh, the irony.

I jump when Rodman gets up and turns the movie off. I look around the stuffy classroom and notice that half of the students are asleep.

I feel an ache of sympathy for this teacher, this man. He doesn't understand this new reality, this changing society of today.

Nothing scares teenagers anymore. Nothing seems to catch their attention.

A shooting?

Those happen every day.

The mafia?

That isn't news.

Blood? Violence? Gore?

It's all around us.

All of us.

Or perhaps Rodman does realize all of this. Maybe, just maybe he wishes yesterday's reality is today's norm.

Happy birthday to me.

Rusty's Personal Journal - Thursday, October 14th

Dude, this isn't good. It's not good at all.

I booked it out of Rodman's class about ten minutes ago. Now I'm waiting for the bus that goes downtown to Steve's. I can't believe this crazy blonde bitch is at his place right now.

How does she even know where he lives?

Last I heard, Steve said she started taking a can of mace out of her pocket and was throwing shit all over his apartment.

The next thing will be that damn whip she tried to seduce me with. Why do I have to deal with this? He can't just kick her out?

I'll tell my dad that I went to the gym after school.

Shit, I need another little yellow pill.

Rusty's Personal Journal - Later

It's 5 PM. And I just got home in time for dinner. That shit was so intense. It's gonna be hard to act calm in front of my parents and Frankie of course. Perfect little Frankie.

I love my little bro. Sometimes I wish I was him.

So here's what went down: I get to Steve's apartment and the first thing I notice is the open door and the gaping hole kicked through it. I also immediately hear my crazy blonde ex screaming the following at Steve.

"Why the fuck did you call him?! Just give me my money back and we're good."

As soon as I was spotted, there was silence. Steve was sitting on his leather couch adorned with cigarette burns while my crazy blonde ex stood over him holding the can of mace Steve had spoken of. Steve's eyes were tearing so I assumed she already used it.

"Okay, what's going on?" I asked in exasperation.

"Oh look who it is," crazy blonde ex said. "It's the guy who used me. It figures you two are friends."

"Steve, what's going on?" I said completely ignoring her.

"She says I sold her bad weed. She's tripping. I sold you the same shit. Tell her."

"Listen," I said turning to her. "You need to chill the hell out. Steve's weed is fine, actually better than fine. It's pretty dank. And he's not giving you your money back. This isn't customer service at the supermarket. This is life. And sometimes you just have to face it instead of making excuses."

She looked at me with crazy eyes. I had no idea what this psycho was going to do next. But instead, she did the unthinkable. She listened.

"Just know this," she exclaimed turning to Steve, ignoring me. "I am blacklisting you."

And with that, she threw the can of mace against his mandala tapestry hanging on the wall and left.

"Dude," Steve said getting up while handing me a packed joint. "This one is on me. I know you've got my back."

"Nah man," I replied shaking my head. "Keep it."

And then I left.

I went to the Facebook app on my phone as I was leaving to get my mind off of what I just dealt with.

It's Her birthday. I had totally forgotten.

So I wrote on Her timeline of course:

"Happy Birthday. Don't do anything I wouldn't."

Now I'm laughing at the irony of that post.

Friday, October 15th

Reality produces a much shriller scream than that of fantasy. No one really screams when it comes to fantasy horror; at least I don't.

This may be the reason why I was laughing as Jive, Drunk Pete, and I ventured through the man-made entertainment contraption of what yesterday's folk like to call a "spook house." Tonight, I appeared to be the drunk one.

In other news, Father Monster was on his best behavior last night, greeting all of my relatives with a prescription pill-induced grin.

Oh, the theatrics.

Anyway, my gifts were pretty rad: money, clothing, a new phone, gift cards, and of course, my favorite tea.

But something, rather, someone was missing.

Him.

The man who sang the songs to my heart.

Kiedis.

I miss his smelly truck and hard kiss.

Where's he been anyway?

I mean, he hasn't texted me in days.

But I have noticed one thing: Ugly Girl and her sidekick, Miss Oink, have been ignoring me for a few days now.

Perhaps they've found a new outlet to express their insecurities.

Art?

Boxing?

Schoolwork?

These thoughts are erased from my temporary paper of optimism.

These girls are a product of today's feeble-minded youth, reliant on technology, on society.

They are mosquitoes.

"Hellooo?" Jive waves a hand in front of my face. "Your pizza is getting icky cold."

Thank you, Jive for bringing me back to the present.

My birthday pizza.

"You know in Italy they eat pizza at room temperature," I reply taking a bite of the saucy goodness.

"Word, I've heard that actually," says Drunk Pete taking yet another chug of his bagged can of beer.

"And you know what I've heard?" says Jive's other friend, Ron, who had just walked in. "If you drink any more beer, your piss will start smelling like it."

"Trust me," replies Drunk Pete without denial. "It already does."

"Ew," I answer between chuckles.

We're all laughing at this point, including Ron's pretty, tattooed girlfriend, Katrina.

We all have our baggage though. We ALL do.

Pete's is easy to figure out.

Jive is a genius and does nothing with his life but smokes weed.

Ron is a recovered heroin addict.

Katrina has always stood by him. I'm sure she has baggage of her own.

As for myself, I have a monster father and little trust for anyone.

"So, what do you guys know about this Kiedis guy?" I ask with curiosity.

"The dude is a crazy partier," he replies with his hippy laugh taking another slice.

"The parties he's thrown after shows are brutal," Drunk Pete adds.

I give both of them a puzzled look. I know the dude likes his weed, but really?

Jive automatically reads my look.

"You don't want to know. It's your birthday party."

As they say, ignorance is bliss. But now, I'm curious. Kiedis' shadiness is making me wary of him. Yet he's looking more attractive than ever. Silly, silly me.

Rusty's Personal Journal - Saturday, October 16th

I have to be at the school in 15 minutes aka 9:00 AM. I'm sitting in traffic while my mom lectures me about how this game is very important and blah, blah, blah.

It's the last game of the season.

Thank God.

This is not my thing. Everyone's always like, "Rusty, you're so good, man. This will take you far if you keep going with it."

And then they turn to my dad and they're like, "Put this on his college application. It'll save you some bucks." And then everyone starts laughing like they're high.

Maybe they are high.

But lately, I've been low.

Saturday, October 16th

Life is ironic.

My sister and I are total opposites. Yet people who don't know us think we're twins.

It's ironic.

Anyway, I am currently at the last baseball game of the season, the "big one." My sister is with her friend while I "supervise." I get to sit on cold, metal bleachers in the autumn air, while my sister has a blast cheering on her boyfriend with her friend. I'm sipping the strawberry lavender tea I got for my birthday.

Kiedis and I have also been flirtatiously texting each other.

Yes, he texted me first.

But I wish this game would just start. It's already fifteen minutes late. Apparently, the late start is due to the "star pitcher" being delayed due to some sort of "traffic jam" getting here.

"Who does this guy think he is anyway? He's that great that they can't start without him?" I exclaim.

"Oh my God," my sister replies rolling her eyes at me. "This is the final game! If we win this, we place first in state."

"Yeah, this dude will basically guarantee the winning spot for us," adds her best friend in rapid defense.

I widen my cat eyes and put my hands up

in mock surrender.

Okay then, I thought. I guess I shouldn't have said anything.

Between this wonderful tea and the steamy text messages Kiedis has been sending me, this game isn't that awful so far, even though it hasn't started.

Kiedis- I'd like to lick that tea clean off your body right now. ;)

Me- Oh would you?

Kiedis- You know you'd like it.

Me- No comment

Kiedis- Psh, you suck. So when are we smoking?

Me- Uh… I don't smoke. You know that.

Kiedis- Have you ever tried it?

Me- No and I'm not planning on it silly face.

Kiedis- Fine, no pressure Miss Good Girl.

Me- That's me. Take it or leave it babe.

Kiedis- Meet me after the game?

This is an interesting last minute date to say the least…

But why is it so sudden and so impromptu? What are Kiedis' true intentions?

But before I can think this further, a revolting sight catches my eye: the "star

pitcher." I turn around, rub my eyes, and
look again to make sure this tea wasn't
laced with hallucinogens. It wasn't. I'm not
dreaming or tripping.

The crowd begins to roar with cheer as
Rusty approaches the pitcher's mound, ready
for action.

Later

Rusty is the "star pitcher."

What's wrong with this world?

Since when does a stoner play a sport, let alone baseball?

And the better question is, where are Rusty's lost boys?

His crew?

His apparent friends?

Maybe they aren't his friends.

The weed is their idol.

What if none of us have friends?

What if we're all essentially alone?

Not lonely, rather alone.

The lonely souls are wise. They know everyone on this earth is alone.

My epiphany of the day.

But perhaps I already knew this.

"Woahhh!" roars the crowd.

"What?" I whisper to myself. I sit open-mouthed in both surprise and disgust.

"Shocking isn't it?" says a middle-aged man sitting next to me.

"Huh?"

"But it's also wonderful," he continues.

"The kid's finally reforming himself."

"Rusty?" I ask in confusion. "You mean the pitcher?"

"Yeah, he was out for the first half of the season. He needed to recover. Just look at him now."

Is this guy kidding? Rusty is no better than he was a few months ago. As they say, once a stoner always a worthless stoner. It's a given.

"No offense sir," I retort. "But the guy you're talking about hasn't reformed himself."

"He's got a long way to go," the man nods in agreement. "But he has made some progress."

I wonder if I have a scrunched, confused expression on my face at this point. As if reading my mind, the man turns to face me. His short, black hair, slightly wrinkled, olive skin, and his surprisingly chiseled body seem slightly familiar in a strange way.

Have I met this man before?

"My name's James," says the man. "I know Rusty very well."

"Yeah, and so do I; he's my ex-boyfriend. We broke up because of his addiction to prescription pills and marijuana."

"I know all about that," James proclaims with a slight twinkle in his eye. "I'm his father."

My mind has just been blown.

Rusty's Personal Journal - Sunday, October 17th

I can't believe it. My dad met Her yesterday.

Why was she even there? Was she there to watch me?

Maybe there is still something there… between us. But shit, her sister was there. That's why. Her sister's boyfriend is on the team.

Of course. She would never chill at a baseball game.

Never. I think.

Dude, I need to smoke a bowl and forget this.

Sundays suck.

Monday, October 18th

The zombie halls of the zombie school seem distant from me today.

I notice Ugly Girl and Miss Oink aren't clinging to Rusty. They've been quite distant lately. Let the fates keep it that way.

I didn't meet Kiedis after the baseball game. Let the boy chase me like a pauper does for his future princess.

That was a feisty analogy...

Speaking of feisty, if I were an animal, I'd be a fierce pussycat. My claws would always be out. My bright, violet eyes would beam with hypnotic rays of light that would only lure the good cats in. The self-righteous conformist pussies would turn away not being able to handle my fierce beams of light.

Scratch.

Tap.

Pounce a rat.

There goes the pussycat.

Halloween is in less than two weeks. Jive invited me to Huck's party on Facebook. It's a costume party.

Dressing as a cat would be too easy.

Rusty's Personal Journal - Friday, October 22nd

Halloween is a little more than a week away. Steve is having a party at his place. Normally, I would totally be down to go. Paul is gonna be there and the rest of my crew. But something is telling me not to go.

Dude, I don't know why I've been feeling this way lately. There's a name for this sort of thing... intuition I think?

It's funny. I think I may want to take little Frankie trick or treating this year.

I wonder what she's doing... probably writing in that damn journal.

Sunday, October 31st (HALLOWEEN)

All of the freaks come out at night, especially on Halloween night, Hallow's Eve. The difference is that I'm a freak myself who lets her flag fly every day.

I'm dressed in a sexy little onyx and white corset with a black tutu, fishnets, and my Doc Martens. Artificial blood covers my chest, neck, and parts of my face. The blood covers my zombie bites. My cat eyes are intensely dark tonight. I'm a sexy zombie chick for the evening, ready to bite.

I even convinced my sister to accompany me to the party tonight which is so not her scene. She's friends with Huck's sister. My little sissy is dressed as a cowgirl... typical sister. She's the preppy one who appears normal and isn't. She's the popular girl, president of the French club, gets straight A's, and has the psychotic temper of Father Monster.

She's my sister; and I love her.

But she's just as much of a freak as I am, if not more.

But to onlookers, I'm the eccentric, alternative sister.

I'm the freak.

"I'm driving home tonight," she states in a stern tone as we exit my car. "Hand over the keys, now."

My sister doesn't drink. She doesn't like to lose control; or perhaps she fears it.

One can never tell.

"Fine," I comply as I hand her my lanyard with the keys attached. "I'm not drinking a lot though."

She just rolls her eyes at me as we begin to descend Huck's steep driveway.

"Okay, I think I need to call Jive so we don't get lost," I suggest. My sister agrees.

The steep driveway overlooks Huck's immense backyard. I don't see the trail Jive spoke of.

The sky has an ironic appearance tonight. Fluffy clouds bombard the scenery while the full moon graciously provides illumination.

How can cloudy moonshine exist? How can it appear gloomy when light is right there all along?

A few minutes later, Jive comes stumbling up the grassy yard with flashlights and another tall hippy dude in tow. Jive is clearly drunk… already. It's only 10 PM. He's dressed as a hippy, too easy.

"This is my friend, Don," says Jive introducing me to the tall, lanky hippy holding the other flashlight. I introduce myself to Don as we continue down the foliage. Don isn't in costume. I'm surprised Jive hasn't yet fallen, considering how much he's tripping as he walks.

"How far into the woods are we going?" asks my sister crossing her arms.

"Not much further," Jive replies in his tranquil tone.

But in reality, I'm thinking the same thing. It seems as if we've already walked ¾ of a mile.

Wait.

I see fire.

I see glowing, orange embers.

I begin to smell a delicious aroma of burnt wood mixed with wine. We're only a few yards away from the party. I see people in costume. I hear drunken chatter, laughter, and someone yelling, "Don't do it!" A second later, Huck runs and jumps over the three foot fire.

"We have arrived," Don proudly announces while taking a swig at his bottle of beer.

* *

My sister immediately left the party to hang out with Huck's sister. I'm halfway through my second cup of Huck's homemade mead. It tastes like a mixture of fresh honey straight from the hive with a hint of cinnamon. Mead is the only wine I'll drink because it's so sweet.

"Enjoying the mead?" asks Huck who is dressed as a Viking. But really, Huck does look like a Viking.

Tall.

Long, thick hair.

Beard.

Big-boned.

Huck.

Viking.

Grrr.

"It's yummy," I answer, starting to feel the mead kicking in. "Thanks for making this."

"I'm glad," he says with a smile.

Huck and I continue to talk about nonsense. Jive and Don join in our conversation of mead and other elixirs. When all of a sudden, someone who had just arrived pulls me away from the drunken chatter, the blissful nonsense.

Kiedis is here.

He's dressed as a vampire.

This vampire is about to get bitten.

Rusty's Personal Journal - Monday, November 1st

Trick-or-treating with little Frankie was actually not that bad. Most people gave me candy too, which was cool. It made me think about being a kid Frankie's age again. I wish things were still that simple. Frankie got tired mad early though, and we were back home by 9 PM.

Steve hit me up and asked if I was coming through. I told him, "nah." I had all that I needed: my candy, my weed, and every horror movie known to man.

It was probably one of the best Halloweens I've had in a while.

A lot of people aren't in school today.

Damn, am I the only one who didn't get wasted last night?

What am I turning into?

Am I the monster?

Or are they?

Monday, November 1st

I feel like a zombie. But it was worth it. I'm just going in for Rodman's class today.

Sister is pissed off.

Mama understands.

Father Monster has no clue.

Tuesday, November 2nd

As cliché as it sounds, love is in the air.

He is love, sunshine, a unique flower blowing in the wind. I feel the light, fluffy petals in my hands. The petals have a smooth feel. The stem feels firm in my palm, ready to share its unique juice with whomever it wants. I kiss the flower. I curiously taste its nectar. He's my flower, my nectar of seduction.

He is Kiedis.

It's quite difficult for me to pay any attention to teachers today. Every thought seems to come back to Kiedis. My choral teacher just asked me if I was feeling alright. That's how dazed I appear.

Huck's party was one of the wildest nights I've ever experienced. (I mean wild in a good way of course.) Now that my mind is defogged I can recall the events from Huck's party.

As soon as I caught sight of Kiedis the Vampire, my cheeks automatically filled with heat. This was not due to the three foot fire. The memory of our short but very intimate kiss induced this heat.

I began walking closer to Kiedis. He was talking to Ron and Katrina. The closer I got to Kiedis, the more I could see how high he was. Like myself, Kiedis had fake blood on his face and costume. I was already verging on drunk.

"Hey," I said with an uncontrollable grin. "I like your costume."

"Oh hey," Kiedis answered with a full bottle of beer in hand.

Kiedis' eyes were glazed over; and his lips were doing that sexy pouty thing again. Boy, did I want this vampire's blood...

"You look so high, Kiedis," I giggled not knowing what else to say.

"And you, look like a naughty little zombie girl," he sloppily rebutted grazing his finger under my chin. "You're supposed to be Miss Good Girl."

"I can be bad for one night. It's Halloween, Mr. Obvious."

"Hey, I think you got some of my vampire blood on your face," Kiedis mumbled taking a swig of beer.

"Oh my God, where is it? Get it off!"

"It's where I touched you just now," he spit out through hysterics of drunken laughter.

I rubbed my face in desperation.

"Hey Katrina?" I asked as she was right next to me. "Is there any vampire blood right here?" I pointed to my chin.

"Yeah, Kiedis got you good," she said straightening the halo on her angel costume.

"Freakin' idiot boys," I added crossing my arms.

"You're telling me," she replied rolling her eyes. "Look at Ron right now."

Ron, Huck, Jive, Don, and Kiedis were dancing around the fire howling like banshees.

Katrina and I couldn't contain our laughter any longer.

"Join us!" Jive yelled pointing to both of us.

And we actually did. This is what the excessive consumption of mead does to a person.

The rest of Huck's guests were staring at us with both confusion and amusement. But I liked the attention. It didn't at all faze me.

I grabbed hands with Katrina on my left and Jive on my right. We ran faster and faster around the three foot fire. The glowing orange flames began to morph into a crimson... then a pale yellow... followed by flamingo pink. The woods, the rainbow fire, and the ironic moon and clouds became a scenic panorama. The panorama was surrounding me, my being. The happiness in everyone's eyes was contagious. I felt it enter my own within seconds of our drunken dance. For once in my life, I not only felt free, but I felt a sense of unity with my peers.

Were these my friends?

Was I actually gaining a new sense of friendship?

Or will I be hit like an innocent doe crossing the parkway?

Stop the paranoia.

Live in the present.

Enjoy the now.

And that is what I did for once.

I didn't overthink.

I embraced the panorama.

I danced in it, literally.

A few moments later, the seven of us droned to a sway like a carousel slowly coming to a halt. We dropped onto the chairs surrounding the fire pit and welcomed the dizziness. Once we came to our senses, conversation erupted once again.

"Guys, I have an idea," I stated feeling spontaneous. "Let's play Truth Is."

"Let's do it," Katrina agreed.

"Lame," Ron yelled out.

"What are we doing?" asked Drunk Pete who had just walked over and looked as drunk as ever. He was also sniffling… excessively.

"A lame high school game, you cokehead," Ron answered with a put-on smile.

Ron is clearly a smart ass, obnoxious type of drunk.

"Uh, well it was just an idea. We don't have to play," I added feeling the rejection.

"Nah, nah," Jive interrupted. "I wanna play. We're playing."

"We'll go in round robin order," I announced. "I'm first. Okay Don, truth is you seem like a rad dude even though we just met."

I figured I would start with a light one... But Don thought otherwise.

"Okay, Katrina, truth is, if you weren't with Ron, I'd bang the hell out of you," he started cracking up.

Katrina sat there with her mouth in an "o" shape.

Awkward.

Ron looked like he might punch Don's lights out.

"Dude, I was joking. Chill."

Then we all laughed about it.

It was Katrina's turn.

"Jive, truth is, I really wish you would get your psychology degree already because my boyfriend is in desperate need of help," she smirked sticking her tongue out at Ron.

I giggled. They were too funny.

"Okay," Jive began pointing to Kiedis. "Truth is I need my weed. Where is it, Kiedis?!"

Kiedis popped a handful of joints out of

his vampire cape in response.

"I was feeling generous, so one for each of you," Kiedis slurred as if he was Santa Claus giving out dolls and toy cars to the good children.

But these were naughty children.

Or were they?

I curiously watched as everyone took their own joint. And then there was one left. I looked around the circle at the fourteen eyes staring back at me. There was nothing but the sound of distant partiers and the crackling of the fire.

"Ever tried marijuana, little girl?" asked Kiedis with an irresistible smirk.

"Uh…" Everyone in the circle was giggling.

"If it's your first time, it probably won't affect you," Katrina reassured me, putting her tattooed hand on my bare arm.

I was already pretty wasted.

I had had around three glasses of mead. That was a lot for a girl my size. I've never tried smoking weed. Then a thought came to mind: *You only live once.*

It was Halloween.

I could be bad for one night.

The next thing I knew, I had grabbed the joint from Kiedis' hand. I slid the end through my lips while Kiedis lit it up. The

smell of weed was nothing new to me though.
Every show or concert I go to people around
me smoke it. But the taste of that herb was.
It was strong… But I liked it.

But then someone else came to mind:
Rusty. Rusty likes weed too. I'm a good
girl. I'm not like Rusty. I don't want to
be.

And then I had a coughing fit, which made
Kiedis laugh even more. Thoughts about Rusty
suddenly vanished.

"You'll get used to it little girl,"
Kiedis commented walking over to my side of
the fire.

Everything that happened after that was
blurry to me except for one thing: Kiedis
and me.

I was walking to Huck's house to go to
the bathroom. Kiedis was next to me, holding
my hand on the muddy trail. My hands were
cold; but Kiedis had warm, soft hands that
heated my entire body up. I couldn't stop
shivering. The night had gotten cold.
Everything was spinning. I felt the bliss
leaving and the hangover entering at
whatever time this was.

The bathroom light was way too bright for
my liking. I urinated, but surprisingly
didn't vomit. The next thing I knew I was
laying on a reclining couch on top of
Kiedis. Our bodies felt so warm together. He
stopped my shivering somehow. To me, it felt
like magic.

We were gazing into each other's eyes. I

felt his hand grab my butt. I giggled. He
bit his lip with his fake vampire fangs. I
felt hot all over and my cheeks turning a
darker shade of red. I felt the force
between us building until we couldn't handle
it any longer.

I kissed him with fervor. And he
aggressively responded. Soon, we were full
on making out. Tongues were fighting each
other in their own game. I felt like I was
floating.

It didn't feel like we were at Huck's
party anymore. Kiedis and I were having a
party of our own. And I didn't want this
party to end.

When he started to touch me, I let him.

I even retaliated.

I was quite the feisty zombie girl.

We explored each other all over.

I was definitely in love.

Kiedis was and still is my love.

And I'm his.

Rusty's Personal Journal - Thursday, November 4th

There's something different about Her. She's still always alone and she still writes in that damn journal.

But dude, there's something weird going on with Her.

She's smiling.

Her eyes have been looking spaced out lately.

Anyway, Steve has become so damn annoying. All he wants to do is chill at his apartment and smoke from his bong and watch old cartoons. But I'm just not feeling it anymore.

I wanna do things. I don't want to work in retail after high school or deal drugs or live with my parents. Dude, I hate to say it but things need to change.

Wait... I figured Her out.

Holy shit.

She started smoking weed.

I don't think she even knows who she is anymore.

But who am I?

Friday, November 5th

Kiedis and I are going on a date to the coffeehouse tonight.

The weird thing is, after all the time we've been seeing each other, I know barely anything about him.

This should be a revealing night for us both.

My mother and I are lying to Father Monster about who I'm seeing tonight. I don't like to lie, but it's what has to be done around my monster of a dad. He would give us hell if he knew I was seeing a guy, especially one that looks like Kiedis.

Wish me luck.

Later

I'm home now. It's just about midnight. And I don't know what to think about Kiedis anymore. I don't know who to believe.

Where did he get his information from?

NO ONE besides my mom and sister know about Father Monster and his hellish antics, his sadistic ways.

When I had arrived at the coffeehouse, I spotted all of the regulars, the guidos, guidettes, and the smoke. I ordered my usual chai latte infused with coconut syrup. Its taste made me long for summer.

But that reminded me of something.

Kiedis never paid for me. Ever. Not once.

Money isn't the turn-off though.

It's simply the principle, a mere one of the many rules that help to compile the Book of Chivalry. Kiedis broke most if not all of those rules.

Kiedis is a bad boy, a rocker in a band called Spoiled Tulips.

Rules are nonexistent to a guy such as himself.

Anyway, Kiedis arrived after twenty minutes of my sitting by myself. Jive and the others were outside. I had said "hi" as I entered the coffeehouse; but I just didn't feel like talking to them at that moment. I had butterflies in my stomach. I wanted to kiss Kiedis some more and feel his smooth abs on mine like we did at Huck's party.

"Hi," I smiled like a little girl.

Kiedis just nodded his head and gave me a quick hug hello in response. He felt slightly damp with perspiration. His cheeks were also flushed a light shade of baby pink.

He wasn't high though. He just seemed…

Nervous?

Uncomfortable?

Something like that.

It was odd.

I had sensed that something was the matter, but I tried to play it cool at first.

"So what were you up to today?" I asked as we sat down at the corner table.

"Just hung out with a few friends," he bluntly answered taking a swig of his large iced coffee.

"Nice, I just watched a movie and went for a walk," I replied. "Maybe we can go walking somewhere some time."

"Mhm."

"So who were you hanging out with anyway?"

"I don't think you know them," Kiedis answered nervously, looking away from me and towards the coffeehouse entrance.

"Everyone knows everyone around here," I sarcastically replied, rolling my eyes. "Nothing is surprising to me anymore."

And that was, and still is the truth. People are truly crazy in this world.

But what had come out of Kiedis' lips at the next moment felt like a splash of ice water to the face.

"I heard about your father," he blurted out in a matter-of-fact manner.

I stumbled for words for a few seconds. I began to feel a wave of cold sweat come over me. Anxiety was starting to take over. And it was very difficult to control. But I had to keep composure.

No one could find out about Father Monster.

No one.

The consequences would be unspeakable.

Seriously, I have to play this off, I had hastily thought in those few seconds.

"What are you talking about?" I inquired with my best attempt at the most serious expression possible.

"I know he's psycho," he replied nonchalantly as if having a psycho father was an everyday thing.

"And your point is?" I asked crossing my arms neither confirming nor denying it.

"I have a lot on my plate with Spoiled Tulips... And there's a lot of money I owe to people."

Drug dealers, I felt like coughing but didn't.

"Well yeah," I answered. "I have a lot on my plate too with school and stuff."

"It's like I like you a lot," he continued barely making eye contact with me. "And you're one of a kind. You're kind of amazing. I just don't want your father coming between us."

Woah, woah, woah.

"Okay, who put this shit into your head?" I blurted out in annoyance. I just couldn't pretend I was calm any longer. "My father doesn't even know about us; so that's not a problem."

"I can't say," he weakly replied. "All I know is, I really like you, but I don't know how much longer I can see you."

His positive statements: "You're one of a kind"; "I really like you"; meant nothing to me. He might as well hadn't said them. I couldn't stand to face Kiedis any longer; so I made an excuse to leave.

He didn't even stop me.

Rusty's Personal Journal - Sunday, November 7th

I'm beginning to wonder if anyone in this world is real.

And by real, I mean genuine.

I only turned Steve's plans down once a few days ago and on Halloween. And the next thing I know I'm being mocked by everyone who are supposedly my friends. Steve is calling me a prude. Paul says I'm selling out to society.

Dude, it's not the words that hurt.

It's the disappointment.

Maybe they were smoking my joint, not enjoying the ride with me, but enjoying the ride without me.

What is a friend anyway?

Even though a lot of businesses close early today, I'm going out to search for a few part-time jobs, something to keep my mind occupied from all of the bullshit.

Fuck Sundays, man.

Monday, November 8th

I'm a strong believer in fate. What's meant to be will be.

But the more I think about what Kiedis said, the angrier I get. It's hard for me to focus on any of my classes today. But I am.

I'm the good girl who gets A's in all her subjects. I'm the girl who's polite to her elders. But I'm also the girl who's enamored with a douchebag named Kiedis. I always seem to fall for them.

Before Kiedis there was Rusty who is just as bad.

Ugh. I need to get Rusty out of my thoughts and these journal entries.

At least this weekend was actually a real one for me this time. Father Monster was in his rare but happy form. He decided to take all of us up to the country for lunch and shopping. Father Monster is a pretty funny dude when he's not a monster; but that's what he is: a monster. I never forget that.

When my mom and I were alone in Hot Topic I reminded her. I said, "You know this isn't going to last. You do realize that."

"Yeah, I know," she said as we both looked through the rack of clearance band t-shirts.

I had bought a band t-shirt on sale and a pair of fake plugs… with Father Monster's money that he gave me. My philosophy is to use the system. In that instance, it meant use the Father Monster while it's in happy mode.

I don't abuse the system.

I use the system.

I'm in Rodman's class now. He's ten minutes late, but just walked in. He automatically caught my attention when he announced something to us.

"Today we will be discussing the notorious crime couple, Bonnie and Clyde. They may have been criminals; but they loved each other through it all. Any questions before we begin?"

I had a weird feeling.

I had to ask, so I did.

"Excuse me? But you're never late, Mr. Rodman. Is something the matter?"

A dark look grew in Rodman's crusty eyelids. He suddenly took hold of his cane, which he only uses sometimes. He coughed and responded.

"Well, I was going to wait to announce this; but I will not be back after winter break. I'm going for bypass surgery, which requires a while for recovery."

I sat in disbelief. I didn't want anyone to replace Rodman next semester. He's the best teacher I've ever had. I couldn't find the right words. But someone from the back of the room beat me to it.

"We're going to miss you dude," Rusty

solemnly said as he sat up in his chair for the first time ever.

Rusty's Personal Journal - Monday, November 8th

The amount of time Rodman is taking to get to class right now I can be smoking an entire bowl.

I can almost smell it.

Wait, I do smell it.

Dude, how can anyone in this class be smoking right now?

Wait a minute... the window's open.

Wow what a surprise... It's Steve and Paul smoking a big one outside near the Clear Directions wing in the old alleyway.

I'm glad I'm not in Clear Directions. They almost put me there when I first got cut from the baseball team a bunch of months ago.

But my parents fought that shit and won.

Yes, Rodman's finally here. Time to get on with my day...

"Today we will be discussing the notorious crime couple, Bonnie and Clyde. They may have been criminals; but they loved each other through it all. Any questions before we begin?"

Then I see Her raise her hand.

She looks cute today. She's wearing her pink Doc Martens again and black denim overalls. But dude, she looks more and more depressed every time I see Her. I wonder what's up...

She asks Rodman why he's late.

I can't believe it.

One of the only genuine people I know is getting major surgery and won't be back after winter break.

"We're going to miss you dude," I say with the utmost sincerity.

Because I really do mean it.

I'm going to really miss that dude. I feel like he's the only person in this school with any real wisdom, a sage of sorts who is always receptive to our punk ass suburban commentary.

Wednesday, November 10th

Kiedis wants to see me again this Friday.

It's odd really.

Maybe he actually realizes Father Monster won't get in the way.

Or maybe I'm just too optimistic, too naïve.

My English teacher knows I'm writing. She just gave me the dirtiest look.

Would she rather me consume myself with social media like all of the other mindless trash bags do here?

I write.

I haven't logged in to my Facebook profile in a few weeks.

That should say something to her, to all of these judgmental, ignorant people.

Anyway, I hope Kiedis isn't like the others.

Friday, November 12th

I just got home.

Kiedis can go to hell.

I'm in no mood to write.

Rusty's Personal Journal - Sunday, November 14th

The bowling alley called me yesterday and said they want me to work at the snack bar, making food and other edibles for their (rude) bowlers. I say rude because I was warned by Chris, my manager, and I experienced said rudeness shortly after during tonight's shift.

I mean I'm in training, learning the register, the grill, and all of that other useless garbage. It's my goddamn first day, you know.

I hate to call women names, but this one was a real bitch. So she comes to the snack bar with her obnoxious kids who are pouring sugar all over the counter and screaming. And this woman wants me to make three orders of chicken fingers, one mini pizza, and fries and she wants it as soon as possible. I try my best and I thought everything came out pretty good for a first try.

"It's my first night," I said after she ordered hoping she would understand.

She just nodded in response.

So like ten minutes later when I bring her food out, she claims that the chicken is too dry to eat and that it's inedible.

It was fine so I don't know what her issue was.

So I gave her a refund and I ate the delicious tenders.

People suck man.

This is my first time smoking a bowl in a week.

Thursday, November 18th

Tears of darkness,

streams of salty water make their shiny

paths

trailing down my face;

smudging all remains of my cat eyes.

My soul feels it is lost,

but not forever.

I lick these salty streams every night
before I go to sleep.

Like a mermaid, I swim in my streams of
solace,

comfort.

Momma helps.

She hugs, kisses, loves

as she should.

And I love her too.

But momma needs to know;

I'm a big girl, an ever-evolving mermaid

who needs to find saltless waters,

and drain these streams of darkness

by myself.

Then, I'll be free.

Rusty's Personal Journal - Thursday, November 18th

I just got home from work.

Going to school and working is probably just as tough as playing baseball while in school.

I met one of my co-workers tonight. She's kind of fat and has a bunch of piercings on her face. Oh yeah and half her head is shaved too.

Her name is Fern.

She came in to work tonight to say hi to Chris and brought her friend, Sparrow, with her.

Sparrow is a tall dude with greasy, long hair and a bushy beard who walks around bare foot.

He's basically a dirty hippy, but it's all good. He's a cool dude.

Sparrow was telling me about this meditation thing at his girlfriend's shop this Sunday.

And for some reason I feel like I should go.

Friday, November 19th

It's lunch.

I'm once again eating in my choral teacher's room.

Those guppies can't hang with my mermaid self.

Kiedis is a guppy.

Ugly Girl and Miss Oink are his masters.

They sucked his brain out until he turned mindless under their command.

Ugly Girl wanted her revenge.

But what she didn't and still doesn't understand, is that one can't control the godly forces of young love.

Months ago, when Rusty swam to our shores, he and I fell in love like angelfish.

Ugly Girl was supposed to be with him.

I was to be Miss Matchmaker, which I intended.

But then Cupid gave Rusty and me a visit.

From then on, Miss Matchmaker became nonexistent. Rusty couldn't control his fins; and I couldn't control mine.

When I met Rusty he was a merman.

Now, I have no clue as to what sea creature he is.

All I know is that I am a mermaid.

And that's what matters.

Rusty's Personal Journal - Friday, November 19th

Lunch is overrated man.

So I was just down there eating with Steve and Paul when my crazy blonde ex approaches me and wants to talk in private.

The following was running through my mind:

FUCK FUCK FUCK FUCK FUCK FUCK. NOOOOOOOOOOOO.

So I was like, "To be honest, I don't really feel like talking to you."

Steve and Paul started to laugh. I know to onlookers I was probably acting like a total dick. But if they only knew the situation they would know I was right.

Then I see tears forming in her eyes and she's like, "Why not?"

"I'm with my friends right now," I said trying not to flip out. "You can tell me whatever you want right now."

"Fine," she said crossing her arms. "We're getting back together."

That was when Steve and Paul started laughing harder.

"What?" I was floored. "Where did you get that idea from?"

"Because I know you're still into me," she said bending down so everyone can practically see her tits hanging out of her tank top.

"But I'm not," I said. "You're delusional."

"I'm delusional?! I'm delusional?! Then what the hell was that note that you left on my locker this morning?"

"I didn't leave a note…"

"Oh yes you did," she said whipping it out of her bra.

I opened the note, which read:

Let's meet up after school today, beautiful. Let's forget about the past. Love, Rusty

"Uh, this wasn't me," I said. "I'm sorry."

"Sorry dude," Steve said to me trying not to laugh.

Steve and Paul were practically rolling on the floor at this point. It looked like my crazy blonde ex was about to kill someone.

"You guys are assholes," I said to both of them shaking my head.

Then I left. And here I am now, walking the halls listening to my music and not giving a fuck about anything.

I have no true friends anymore. I never did.

But then something stops me and I take my earbuds out.

I see Her in the chorus room, eating lunch by herself.

Now I know why she never comes to the cafeteria.

Sunday, November 21st

I finally went on Facebook today. Jive invited me to this meditation event at his friend Luna's shop. I'm leaving with him in a few minutes. This is sure to be hippy central.

But I'm down for any enlightenment right now.

I need to let go.

Later

And hippy central it was indeed.

Luna's shop sells belly dancing skirts, all-natural mineral makeup, hookah, incense, chakra crystals, cute jewelry, and other New Age stuff. It was kind of rad though.

Jive and I walked up a flight of stairs to a room adorned with elaborate tapestries. Luna was smudging the room with a sage stick to "cleanse the air of negative energy." A few women around my mom's age, Luna, Luna's boyfriend, a chunky girl with a bunch of facial piercings, Jive, and I were all sitting in a circle together while relaxing bongo music played from a stereo by the stairs.

Luna is anti-technology. She doesn't own a phone. But who could blame her? She told all of us to turn our phones off during the meditation.

Anyway, it was almost time for the meditation to begin. When all of a sudden, I heard the thump of footsteps from someone walking up the staircase. I should have known. It's like I can't go anywhere without seeing him lately. Yes, you guessed it: Rusty.

Rusty. Rusty. Rusty.

Is he stalking me? Since when does this guy meditate? First I learn he plays baseball, and now he meditates? What's next? Does the new "reformed" Rusty read stories to little kids? Does he volunteer at the animal shelter? It wouldn't surprise me at this point; though nothing really does anyway. This is such an act, seriously.

He probably smokes weed with Luna, I thought to myself as he walked into our circle.

I couldn't help but to smirk at the very possible and likely thought that Rusty is acting like a good, well-behaved, respectable teenager. I clasped a hand over my mouth to keep from bursting out in laughter.

"Oh hey," Rusty casually nodded to me as he sat down next to fat piercing girl and Luna's boyfriend.

I was about to ask what he was doing at the meditation when Jive interrupted.

"You okay? What's so funny?"

"Nothing," I said looking right at Rusty with a smile as everyone held hands. "Everything's cool."

And the meditation began.

Rusty's Personal Journal - Sunday, November 21st

She was there.

I never believed in that New Age shit until a few hours ago.

As cheesy as this sounds, it was like I was meant to see her there at the meditation.

Not gonna lie, it was pretty hard to focus on "drifting out of my physical body" when all I could think about was Her.

Dude, I don't know what's happening to me lately. First, I was forced into re-joining the baseball team, which I actually turned out to like, then, I started bailing on my bros, then, I cut back on my weed intake, and now, I'm falling for my ex again.

Maybe Paul is right. Maybe I am selling out to society.

My mind is spinning, man.

And I don't think it's from the hookah we all smoked after the meditation at Luna's shop.

Monday, November 22nd

So I'm waiting for Rodman's class to start. And famous criminals are the one thing not on my mind right now. Something odd happened earlier today.

I didn't eat alone in the chorus room during lunch. I had brought a cheddar broccoli soup from home, my favorite kind of soup. I slurped the first steamy spoonful and was savoring it after a long few hours of schoolwork.

My slurping was interrupted by a distant sound. But I didn't even mind being interrupted mid-slurp. That's how beautiful this sound was.

It was an acoustic guitar strum, a familiar melody. And it was coming from a room over: the band room.

No one is ever in there at this time, I thought.

Curiosity made me do it.

I swear.

As I slowly crept closer and closer, soup in hand, the beautiful melody became clearer and clearer to me. Someone was playing my favorite song.

I was almost afraid of who the mystery musician might have been at that moment. My mind was telling me not to look, but my curious heart said to go for it.

I looked.

And he noticed.

I continued to stare.

And he continued to play and mumble the song lyrics.

These lyrics aren't meant to be mumbled; the quality of one's voice doesn't matter, I thought.

If he sang like he played... well, just maybe my heart would cave for him. Maybe.

But I'm not stupid.

I remembered the past between Rusty and me. His parting words swam through my mind as I watched him strum the beautiful song.

"She's just making this miserable for the both of us. I think it's best if we both take a break. It's just too much drama, babe. Sorry."

Just like that, we were done.

And we have been ever since.

All because of Ugly Girl.

All because of dumb, young love.

All because of Rusty's stupidity.

I was initially angry that he would be that weak-minded.

But since then, the fog has drifted. Rusty became a stoner. I became a recluse punker chick with the good girl exterior.

But that was eight months ago.

Wait.

The strumming had stopped.

I looked up from under the ocean of my swimming thoughts.

I met his dark eyes of hurt, maybe regret too.

Without even realizing it, I had entered the band room. I was about ten feet away from Rusty.

"That's my favorite song," I numbly stated.

"I know," he replied looking down at his guitar. "I was hoping you'd hear it."

"Give me a break," I said rolling my eyes. "I saw you kissing you know who a few months ago. Admit it. You're hooking up with her. Don't play with my head. I'm in no mood."

"And so what if I was hooking up with her?"

"It's a dumb choice, Rusty. You've made a lot of dumb choices since we broke up. But it's not my problem that you turned into a stoner! Remember all of the poetry you used to write and the band you had? What the hell happened, Rusty? Please, enlighten me."

"I don't have a real answer," he shrugged.

"Maybe you don't know the answer," I replied standing over him. "Or maybe you do and you're just too afraid to admit it."

"Damn, you were always so deep," Rusty sarcastically responded staring straight into my soul. "The world isn't that simple."

My skin was heating up, boiling lava under the surface. I wanted to slap Rusty across his stoner face. But I also had the urge to pin this boy to the wall and kiss him madly. It was an odd, contradictory feeling. But I liked it.

"You... ugh!" I stumbled for words. "Why do you keep appearing everywhere lately? Are you like following me? What's the deal with that? First, it was the baseball game, then the meditation, and now here. I just want answers, Rusty. Am I going crazy? What's going on?"

I just freaked out at this kid. I thought he was going to leave or walk away like he used to.

But then something strange happened, something I hadn't seen Rusty do in a while.

He stood up and smiled, a full-toothed, adorable smile. And then he said, "You may be a little weird and crazy, always have been, but what if I was following you? Why do you care?"

"What we once had, Rusty... it was great. Then she got in the way. Why..."

I had to take a second to compose myself.

Fuck.

"Why," I continued. "Would you let a jealous bitch get in the way of us?"

Rusty's smile automatically faded. And there was a one second pause that felt infinite.

"Maybe I was those things. Well yeah, actually I pretty much sucked as a boyfriend. I've changed though. I've been smoking less."

"And your point is?" I was growing impatient.

"Well," he said looking down. He began to take a few small steps towards me. He softly held my waist…

and he kissed me.

Just once.

The imprint he left on my lips was truly intense. Even when his plump reds left mine, I felt a sensation as if they were still there.

Then the bell rang.

My mind swam up from under the surface and into the sunny sky.

Rusty's Personal Journal - Tuesday, November 23rd

When the radio sounded from my alarm clock today, I woke up with a purpose.

I'm usually swearing under my breath, pressing the snooze button, and cursing my existence.

But today was different.

We ate lunch together again. It was awesome. I played guitar. She dug it. And we caught up. She told me about what an asshole that guy Kiedis is and I told her all about my crazy blonde ex, who she calls Ugly Girl.

We laughed about that one for a few minutes.

And we plan on meeting again tomorrow.

Thursday, November 25th

It's like eight months ago all over again.

Well, not exactly...

It's not like Rusty and I are dating.

Like I said, I'm not that stupid.

But it just feels like puppy love.

It's like those famous photos of the little boy and girl holding hands near a pond, or like when the boy is handing the girl a rose.

It feels like that except for the fact that Rusty never gave me a rose; and when we hold hands, it's in the dirty, old band room, not a quaint pond.

Not to get too mushy, (excuse me if I already have), but I'm feeling real butterflies, butterflies that make light journeys through my stomach and give me that weak feeling as a result, like a drug.

Ever since Monday, Rusty goes to the band room and plays his guitar. I eat lunch. We hold hands. Not much talking happens, nor does it need to.

I'm not getting my hopes up.

I haven't forgotten the past.

I never will.

But how can someone who scarred me so deeply also give me these butterflies?

It's now that time again: lunch in the band room.

I walk in and find the following:

Vacancy.

Chairs.

Percussion instruments.

Music stands.

Sheet music.

But no Rusty.

Rusty's Personal Journal - Thursday, November 25th

Dude, I don't think I can do this dating stuff. Even though these past few days have been fucking awesome, I remembered what happened last time we did this. My crazy blonde ex/Ugly Girl, as she calls her, really messed things up for us.

I know I'm a strong dude, but I don't wanna go through that heartbreak, that drama, again.

I'm cutting out early today with Steve. I need to think about all of this.

Friday, November 26th

Rusty is absent today.

Or maybe he's just playing sick, like the weak-minded stoner he is.

Either way, I'm so done with him.

Men are pigs.

And Rusty is no exception.

At least the Spoiled Tulips are having a show tomorrow night at the lake house.

Indoors.

Season changes suck.

My creamy orange and fuchsia sky is dead.

Later

FATHER MONSTER HAS ERUPTED.

The cops are here.

I can't stop shaking.

Sister is silent.

Mother can't stop weeping.

I feel like we're all, slowly but surely, crumbling to ashes to nothing but invisible particles in the air.

Family, what a word.

Rusty's Personal Journal - Friday, November 26th

I fucked up yesterday.

I thought I was getting better, but I guess I'm not.

My parents got a call from the school yesterday saying I wasn't there for the second half of the day.

I should have realized that was going to happen.

When Steve picked me up yesterday he took me to the beach at the lake, where The .Spoiled Tulips usually play and are having a big show tomorrow night. It was freezing man, like it had to be 20 degrees, but it was totally deserted so we figured, why not?

So anyway, we walked around smoking a joint Steve had packed before we left. And I was telling him about my dilemma with Her. And he was like, "So what's the big deal?"

And so I was like, "The big deal is, I think she might be special." Then Steve started laughing.

And he was like, "So you're saying you're going to cave and actually throw yourself at this chick? Dude, is it even worth the shit you're going to get from your ex?"

And by ex, he meant my crazy blonde one.

Then I said, "Bro, I don't care about her. I don't care about what any of these other chicks have to say. I think I made my mind up. I don't even know why I came here with you."

And then Steve was all, "Whatever dude, you're crazy."

Well, maybe I am crazy. But maybe I do really like this girl.

Maybe I love her.

My parents said that since I don't think school is important enough, they enrolled me in this eight-hour program for today. I'm going to the county jail and getting lectured about "where I'll end up if I continue on this destructive path."

Fun.

Saturday, November 27th

Fathers are supposed to be loving.

Mine threw a phone at my mom's face after ripping it out of the wall.

Fathers are supposed to believe their children over others.

Mine kicked a hole through my bedroom door and screamed in my face accusing me of telling everyone about how psycho he is… me, the ungrateful, ugly, cunt.

Fathers are supposed to appreciate their loved ones, especially with Thanksgiving being tomorrow.

Mine was chasing my mom around the house threatening to kill all of us if she ever left him.

And finally, daughters aren't supposed to be afraid or fearful of their father.

My sister hid under her bed crying, while I locked myself in the bathroom and dialed 911 from my cell phone, which I hid in my underwear the whole time.

I'm a broken faucet.

Mother and I are disgusted and broken.

Sister bottles everything inside.

Monster is away at the psych ward in the local hospital.

He's no longer my father. If anyone asks, my father is dead, and has been for a long time.

I'm crying.

Water hasn't stopped trickling from my broken faucets.

Later

I've been on my bed crying for close to three hours. Mother tried to comfort me for the first fifteen minutes of my three hour weeping episode. She kept repeating that "everything will be fine."

But it won't be fine. It'll never even be close to fine.

I am emotionally swollen and justifiably irrational. I told her to leave me alone.

And she did just that.

It's 6:33 PM.

The Spoiled Tulips show begins at 7 PM.

I better get ready.

I lazily stumble over to my dresser. I pull out my oversized tie-dye sweatshirt and my ripped up black skinny jeans. I set aside my neon pink Doc Martens as well.

Then I pause in my mundane routine. I look up and catch my reflection in the mirror.

I'm a mess.

My cat eyes are now meaningless scribbles that run down my cheeks. My eyes are so pink that I look high. My hair looks like a rat's nest.

I look like shit.

I put on my rad outfit and wash my hair in the sink.

I also wash my face.

I rid it of all makeup, the smudges, the invisible scars.

My hair looks good even though it's dripping wet.

I don't care.

I put on a little foundation, a pinch of crimson blush, clear lip balm, and liquid liner.

I am letting my natural cat eyes show tonight.

Hello Spoiled Tulips, greetings mindless peers, my name is Hot Mess.

And I'm ready to party.

Rusty's Personal Journal – Sunday, November 28th (2:00 AM)

I'm about to call my dad to come get us. And by us I mean me and Her. Tonight has been interesting.

So I showed up at like midnight and I saw Her in the corner near the stage taking shots of whiskey with Kiedis' groupies. I had to make sure I wasn't tripping first.

Steve was like, "Woah, is that your girl? She's far gone."

And I was like, "Shut up, man."

I knew something wasn't right. She never drank let alone socialized. From then on it was my task to make sure she didn't do something stupid.

Fuck.

"Hey," I said walking over to her. "Is everything cool?"

"Oh hi, Rusty," she said smiling giving me a hug. "I was wondering where you've been."

The other girls started giggling when I came over.

Then she turned to them and said, "This is the one that serenaded me and then left me out to dry a few days ago."

Yep, she was wasted. I had to talk to her alone.

"Listen, can we talk for a sec? I wanted

to let you know-"

"Nah man," she answered. "I'm about to rip Kiedis a new one."

"Yo Kiedis!" she yelled as The Spoiled Tulips started to break down their equipment. "This is the only thing you'll ever get to see tonight!" And she flipped him off.

His groupies started laughing and Kiedis just shook his head and did the same. I heard one of the other guys in the band ask if "this chick was for real." I had to get her out of here.

"Rusty, I think your friend is waiting for you," she said pointing to Steve.

"Nah, he has other things to do," I replied and waved him away.

So then we took a walk in the bitter air outside. I told her about why I haven't been in school the past few days.

"Mhm," she nodded and smiled slightly. She was shivering too.

"Here, take my coat," I said putting it on over her sweatshirt.

"Thanks Rusty, but I don't think I feel so good..."

Then she turned to the nearest tree and let it all out... some of it splashed on my coat. But I didn't care.

I noticed someone started a fire pit near the frozen water. A few people had been sitting by it, but there was still enough room for us. So we walked over to get warm.

And we sat there for a while. We didn't even need to say anything. We sat and watched the fire dance around us.

When she got a little more sober, we smoked a little and she started talking about her father, how she wished he would change. She was really out of it. She started crying. Then I knew it was time to go.

But we'll get through it.

Sunday, November 28th (2:31 AM)

I'm in deep earth right now.

I can barely speak let alone write.

Rusty's dad is driving me home ha, ha.

Rusty is next to me petting my head.

Like what is going on? What is my life?

I am one hot mess.

And I am wasted.

Sunday, November 28th (day)

Last night was pretty much a blur. The last I remember, I was in a car with Rusty.

I just looked at my phone and notice it's almost noon.

I also notice there are fifteen missed calls on my phone ALL from last night.

13 from Mother.

1 from Sister.

1 from Monster.

Rebellion is an understatement as to what last night was like.

I was out of my mind.

I still feel out of my mind even without the whiskey and weed.

I think I smoked with… WOAH.

I smoked with Rusty. WHY?!

I feel like punching myself in the face.

Realization sucks.

I know I made poor decisions last night. But why the hell did I smoke with Rusty the Stoner? What's wrong with me?

Maybe I'll pretend I'm still asleep just so I don't have to hear-

My door just creaked open.

It's Mom.

She comes in with her arms crossed and her eyes welling with tears.

"I'm disappointed. I didn't know I have a daughter like this."

"I'm sorry Mom," I say sitting up in bed. "I don't have answers. You know I don't normally do this."

"If it wasn't for James, Rusty's father, I would have searched for you myself."

"Mom, I'm sorry. I really didn't hear the phone."

I felt my head throbbing. A hangover was definitely kicking in.

She's crying. I hate to see my mom cry. I continue to speak.

"I didn't mean to upset you. I just- I just wish last night never happened. But it did and…" She interrupts me.

"I just got off the phone with your father. He's being let out today around four. It's Thanksgiving. I think we should all talk."

Is this woman kidding me? I'm not by any circumstances talking to him. He's a monster, not my father.

"No," I protest. "I'm not speaking to that piece of shit ever again. Look at your face, Mom. Look at what he did to you!"

I can't control the tears any longer. My faucets begin to uncontrollably leak once again.

"Are you too afraid to leave?! And what about your daughters? I guess you don't care about our happiness and well-being. Do you even know why I acted the way I did last night? You think I would do all of that crap if he hadn't caused us this turmoil?!"

My faucets begin to erupt gushes upon gushes of salty tears. Her faucets are too.

"How can you even think I don't care about you and your sister's happiness? I love you two more than anything in the world. I would give my life for you two. That's why I don't want to see you out with low lives and smoking joints and getting drunk with people who are below you! Where the hell was your good friend Jive through all of this?"

"I- I don't know. Jive was there but I don't..."

She makes a valid point even though I don't want to admit it. Jive should have helped me in some way when I was wasted. All he did was sit around with Drunk Pete, Ron, and Katrina. He was laughing about something the last I remember... But Rusty was a different story.

"Rusty isn't a lowlife though. He may be a stoner; but he is not a lowlife, Mom."

"I never said that," she answers in a calmer tone through tears. "As a matter of fact, your sister made cookies for his father. Before we pick up dad later, I want you to ring his doorbell and let James know that we appreciate what he did. But before you even think about dating Rusty, he needs to stop getting high, whether you like it or not. And don't ever do that again."

"I promise. I won't."

She comes closer and gives me a tight hug.

"I love you and I want the best for you, honey. And I promise everything will be okay."

"I love you too."

I gently weep into her warm embrace.

Later

It was a time to be thankful, time for repentance.

But it hurt.

As I walked up Rusty's long walkway to his front door carrying a colossal plate of chocolate chip cookies, all I heard was the steady pounding of my heart.

I felt so ashamed.

I'm supposed to be the good girl. I know I'm still good. But does Rusty's father know that? I don't want him to think I'm a bad influence. But more importantly, what does Rusty think of me now?

I feel like I screwed things up.

But it was time.

I arrived at his front door adorned with a totally goofy Thanksgiving wreath. I rang the lit up doorbell.

There were footsteps.

Then there were footsteps descending a staircase.

And finally, I was greeted with an open door and Rusty's father, who looked surprisingly relieved to see me.

"Hello."

"Hi, I just wanted to thank you for driving me home last night. I don't remember much; but I do know you helped me out a lot. Here are some cookies my sister made."

Woah, that was a mouthful.

James nodded, taking the plate out of my hands.

"Thanks, but you really didn't have…"

He was about to say something else, but I wanted to tell him more.

"And also, I'm sorry about everything. Last night, I wasn't in the right place. I never do things like what I did last night. I'm not a party girl. I'm a good girl. I just hope you and your son could see that."

Then there was a slightly awkward pause. His expression changed a bit to a look of concern. After what seemed like an eternity, James answered me.

"I understand. I've dealt enough with Rusty's antics to know. Please, come in."

"My mom and sister are waiting in the car. I can only stay for a few minutes."

He nodded with understanding as I stepped inside Rusty's surprisingly neat yet average home. I smelled fresh turkey and gravy heating in the oven. I always pictured Rusty's home as being a mess and him growing up in a dysfunctional family. Maybe they are dysfunctional. But they don't seem that way.

I noticed a middle age woman with beautiful, long black hair sitting on a couch watching TV as I entered.

"It's nice to finally meet you," she said getting up with a twinkle in her eye. "I'm Priscilla, Rusty's mother. I hear about you all the time."

"You do?" I asked in both disbelief and surprise.

"I do. And you're just as pretty as Rusty said you were."

"Thanks," I blushed not really knowing what to say. "But anyway, where is Rusty?"

"Oh, he's in his room packing. He's not too happy right now," Priscilla replied. "I think you're just the person for him to talk to."

"What do you mean?" I asked in confusion as I was lead down the narrow hallway to his bedroom.

Neither of them answered my question. I was left by myself. I gently knocked on Rusty's door.

"Can you just leave me alone?"

"It's me."

I heard a few zipping noises and then he let me in.

Rusty's room was exactly how I had imagined it. Dozens of band posters lined his baby blue walls. Clothes were strewn all over the floor. There was a scent of dirty boy mixed with the slightest hint of marijuana. A gigantic suitcase sat on his mattress.

"What are you doing here?" he asked in grunts of frustration without looking up while he packed. "Wanna watch me leave for the nuthouse?"

I was so confused.

"I have no idea what you're talking about. I came to thank your dad for driving me and..."

He turned to face me and added, "And are you thanking him for this shit too?"

Rusty threw a pamphlet at me that read, "The Sunshine School, Alexandria, Virginia." I felt his burning stare the entire time I viewed the pamphlet. Tears were building in my eyes again.

I looked up from the shiny paper. And to my astonishment, a drop of water ran down one of Rusty's cheeks.

I felt like someone just pushed me off a cliff.

"What the hell is this, Rusty? Why are you going hundreds of miles away to Virginia?" I was biting my bottom lip, trying to hold back what was coming.

"It's a place for me to change, to get clean," he answered in a mocking tone using air quotes. "It's a school for degenerates, babe. I can't believe they're sending me to this damn place."

I stepped closer and sat next to him on his bed.

He actually called me babe for the first time since we broke up.

"How long?"

"As of now, I'll be gone for two months. And that's only if I'm on good behavior. I can't believe this shit. How can they turn around and tell me today of all days on God damn Thanksgiving? I'm leaving tomorrow morning."

He kept shaking his head. And the next thing I knew, he put his head in his hands. If I had bit my lip any harder it would have bled, so I let a few tears drip.

"Rusty, I'm thankful for you. I hope I didn't ruin things between us because of last night."

Now I put my head in my hands too. I never cried in front of him before that. I didn't want Rusty to see me like this.

All of a sudden, I felt an arm on my back, his arm.

I looked up from the darkness of my hands. Tears were still in his eyes. And he was staring straight into my soul.

"You didn't ruin anything. You're still Miss Nerd."

"I am?!" I said laughing through tears.

"Mhm," he nodded gently pulling me in towards his body.

But he didn't need to. The force between us was too powerful to hold back any longer. His soft lips hugged mine. His tongue embraced mine. My whole body felt warm from his touch alone. I felt this buzzing all over. Rusty and I weren't meant to be apart.

We kissed for only a few moments longer, an immeasurable time.

Then I had to leave and he had to finish packing. We waved goodbye. But as I left his room, I felt something strange. My heart felt like it had wings. When I closed my eyes, all I saw was Rusty and that single tear dripping from his broken faucet. I had tasted his tears when we kissed. And I think he tasted mine too.

As crazy as it sounds, we tasted each other. We were one. Waist in waist. Hand in hand. Arms in arms. Neck to neck. Lips to lips.

Rusty and I.

Epilogue (One Month Later)

Life has been weird.

Once a week, as a family, we all go to therapy together. Father Monster is on heavier meds and has been acting calmer. I still feel like Mother should leave him. But that's beside the point.

Overall, things have been better in my normally psychotic household. Christmas was cool. I got a bunch of rad clothes and tickets to a show I want to see.

I do miss Rusty though. I hope he does get better. A letter of his is sitting in front of me. Writing letters is the only way I can communicate with him. I give them to James. And James delivers Rusty's letters to me.

Last I heard, Rusty was miserable at The Sunshine School. Either way, I'm not getting my hopes up. Our potential relationship needs a lot of growing and care until it actually happens. You can't just plant a flower and expect it to bloom the next day without water. Like a flower, Rusty and I need time, love, and care so we can grow.

So in conclusion, I'm totally ready for the ever-spiraling adventures that await me.

Peace and love.

Dear --------,

Thanks so much for the letters and all the work and love you put into them. It really means a lot.

The good news is, I'm starting to get more used to being here.

Your letters are really helping me out. People here are always like, "Who's writing you? I don't get any letters." And today, I showed my friends your picture and they said you're cute. 'Cuz you are. You're adorable. You're such a good girl. And that's what every guy wants, a good girl who will be "bad" only for him.

Anyway, it's really insane that it's been like over a year since we met. I was the new kid who was supposed to be set up with someone else, but then some unexplainable craziness happened and we started dating. Then that got screwed up. From that point on, my mind went through so many changes with all the drugs I experimented with and all the crazy experiences and overwhelming stress I had.

And here we are today. We got closer again. We connected. But now I'm in a nuthouse school for troubled kids. My mind has been clearer though, probably since I haven't gotten high in a month.

When I get out of here, I'm gonna start living, being more serious about making money, and being independent. I'm gonna get a job, work for a month or so, and then start school again. I'm never gonna ask my parents for money again.

And of course, I'm gonna chill with you! Maybe we could develop into more than friends. I really like you, like I like like you. We just gotta take things slow though 'cuz relationships are stressful, especially when you rush into things. We should start off by hanging out, maybe go out to eat on a date (my treat). It sucks to be this far from you and from everyone in my life. I hope I don't get sent to a residential treatment center after this. I'm trying my best here.

I know I've been rambling, but I've also been writing mini-raps to try to get my mind off smoking bud. I'll show you all of them when I eventually get out. Tell your mom and sister I said hi.

Love,

Rusty ♥

PS- I wish I could make it to Rodman's funeral. It's a shame. That dude taught me a lot. But guess what? You did too.

ABOUT THE AUTHOR

Samantha Apicella has always been passionate about writing. She wrote her first story in the first grade and has not stopped since. *Through Her Voice* is Samantha's debut novel and she hopes that readers of all ages will get something valuable out of it. She lives with her family in a little town in New York. She wishes for all of her readers to find their voice.

Made in the USA
Middletown, DE
07 September 2018